M.O.A.B.

A True-Life Fairy Tale
Of The War On Mother Nature

Alexander Gregory

For Johnny, Michael, and Nicky

Prologue

ONCE UPON A TIME, DURING A FIERCE AND terrible war in Southeast Asia, enemy soldiers often hid in the thick jungle of trees more properly called a tropical rainforest. To more quickly find and attack the enemy in their hiding places, a powerful tree-removing device was invented. It was nicknamed the "Daisy Cutter."

The Daisy Cutter was a clever bomb that didn't wait to hit the ground before exploding. Weighing seven and a half tons, which included over six tons of semi-liquid explosive, it was shoved out the back of a cargo plane and parachuted toward earth. Just before striking the ground, it acted like a giant aerosol dispenser, spraying a huge cloud of explosive mist into the air and then igniting it to create a massive blast that instantly leveled everything around it.

The bomb was sometimes used to create instant landing pads for helicopters carrying assault troops into enemy territory. The bomb could obliterate a large chunk of the rainforest without leaving a crater in the ground. Helicopters can't land in craters. In the blink of an eye, the Daisy Cutter annihilated trees and everything else within three hundred yards of ground zero. It was a devastating weapon in a conflict that was called the "War in Vietnam."

Thirty-five years later, at the dawn of the 21st Century, a new and improved version of the Daisy Cutter had been perfected. The achievement was called a "modernization." It weighed eleven tons, measured thirty feet long, and was guided by satellites. It was called M.O.A.B., which stands for Massive Ordinance Air Blast. It was nicknamed the "Mother Of All Bombs" and holds the distinction of being the most powerful non-nuclear bomb on earth.

A week before another war began, this time in the Middle East, M.O.A.B. was exploded in its first live test on a military base in Florida. Once it left the Hercules cargo plane, global positioning satellites guided M.O.A.B. precisely to its target. At six feet above the ground, an explosive mist of powdered aluminum and ammonium nitrate was ignited in a sudden, fiery, gargantuan blast called an "air burst."

The sound was so deafening and the sight so frightening that the military made plans to use M.O.A.B. not only to destroy things, but to create an experience of what they termed "shock and awe" in the enemy. To many it seemed like a valuable weapon for a conflict that was called the "War in Iraq."

A fair number of civilians heard the test-blast of M.O.A.B. They also saw, from a distance, the billowing white mushroom-shaped cloud created by the explosion. For most, the sight was terrifying, but for a longtime drifter who called himself Mal, it was a vision of the future, a vision that left him feeling empty and sad.

Mal hadn't always been gloomy, but the latest stretch of his life hadn't been his favorite. Everywhere he traveled, he saw signs of looming catastrophe. The signs were unmistakable, and the signs were getting him down.

The signs were making Mal dread the future and eroding his sense of hope. The signs were making Mal start to believe that the world was coming to an end, that the human race was marching down the road to Armageddon.

This is the story of what happened to Mal not long after he beheld M.O.A.B.

1

The Survivors

THE LATE AFTERNOON SUN SHOT MISTY,
bright shafts of light, "God's Light" some called
it, through the forest of 2,000-year-old giant
California redwoods, one of the last remaining
stands. Though he hadn't been here for many
years, Mal truly loved this place. The forest was
primordial and magical and mysterious. Its smell
was intoxicating, and made him feel at ease with
the world. For Mal this was a Garden of Eden.

Mal hoped the forest would raise his spirits and
vanquish his sense of doom. He took it as a good
sign that the redwoods were still standing and
hadn't been cut down. These days Mal found good
signs few and far between.

Mal knew about these ancient trees. He knew they were seedlings when Jesus was born, and as tall as a man when Christ was crucified. He knew when the Huns invaded Europe, they had grown a hundred feet tall. By the time of the Crusades, they had reached two hundred feet. As Napoleon's troops attacked Russia, their height had soared a hundred feet more. With the outbreak of World War I, many of the redwoods stood over 350 feet tall. They had survived fires, storms, earthquakes, floods and droughts. They were the largest living things on earth.

Mal didn't look as smart as he was, mainly because of the way he dressed. Well-worn baggy pants, battered old boots, a long canvas coat, and a backpack -- that was his uniform, the uniform of a seasoned traveler.

Mal didn't look as old as he was either, partly because he was lean and fit. Despite his gray hair and beard, he seemed unnaturally youthful. He had an uncanny timeless quality that made it hard to gauge his age. When Mal told folks he'd been roaming the earth for over 2,000 years, no one ever believed him. But it was true. Mal was more than old. Mal was ancient. He was as old as the oldest redwoods in the forest he so loved.

The most striking thing about Mal was his eyes. They were large, expressive eyes. Emerald-colored eyes. They could look like the eyes of a lucky kid on Christmas morning, or they could look like the eyes of someone seeing their dog run over by a car.

Mal's eyes had seen a lot during his time on earth, but he'd never seen a time when things were as bad as now. To him it looked perfectly clear that the world was being ruined. It was making him angrier everyday, and giving him a dim view of his fellow human beings.

Two things about Mal were for sure. He was funny in a quirky, offbeat way, and he had a temper, a temper that sometimes erupted in a volcano of fiery words. His penchant for ranting helped him let off steam, but it sometimes made him seem a little crazy. As far as Mal was concerned, the world was going crazy.

Mal's plan for the night was to find a cave in the trunk of a redwood large enough to sleep in. The charcoal-lined caves are created by lightning fires from which the tree has healed. Some caves extend far into the trunk, but deep roots and nourishing bark keep the tree alive and growing.

The sun had set and the evening mist had turned into a cold thickening fog. It was then when Mal heard a sound in the distance. It was the sound of the wet rotting mulch being compressed on the forest floor.

Mal stood perfectly still and listened. Nothing. Then he heard it again, but closer. Mal didn't move. He just kept listening.

Now, he heard breathing as well as footsteps. Mal slowly, quietly crouched to the ground, his eyes, his ears, his nose on full alert. He noticed the sound of a dew drop hitting a leaf. Then he heard more footsteps, and then a grunt. He couldn't see it, but he knew what it was. A bear, foraging for food.

The damp fog wafted past Mal toward the sounds of the bear. If the bear caught Mal's scent it would probably follow it directly to him.

Mal knew about animals. He knew that with mountain lions, you're supposed to make yourself large to scare them. You're supposed to stand on your toes, lift your arms and yell at the top of your lungs. He knew that folks rarely got a chance to do that because mountain lions usually attacked from behind. Mal also knew that with bears you're supposed to make yourself small and unthreatening. You're supposed to assume the "duck-and-cover" position once taught to school kids in case of an oncoming nuclear attack.

What Mal knew better than anything was to follow his instincts. He sensed that on this night staying crouched by the redwood would probably get him bitten or mauled. So, in a sudden jolt, he took off running into the darkness and fog of the redwood forest.

A few seconds later, he regretted what he had done. In a glance back over his shoulder he saw the bear pursuing him.

"Aaaaaaahhhhhhh!" In his panic, Mal uttered the sound you're supposed to make when you encounter a mountain lion. He knew that bears weren't easily frightened and he began to run even faster. Another quick glance behind him showed the bear gaining ground.

"Huuuuh!" Mal grunted in pain as he stumbled over a branch and fell face first onto the forest floor. He could hear the bear panting, getting closer.

Suddenly, from high above, a light shined onto Mal. He rolled onto his back and stared into the beam that shot straight down from the redwood tree next to him. Then, the end of a climbing rope banged into his face. He quickly stood up, grabbed it, pulled it taut, and used it to clamber up the trunk of the massive tree.

He had struggled about twenty feet up, when the light shut off and he heard a voice, a woman's voice.

"Just hold it right there," she said.

"Who are you?" shouted Mal up into the darkness.

"Who are *you*?" the voice asked back.

"I'm Mal."

"So, Mr. Mal, are you with the County Sheriff's office?"

"No. No. I don't have an office."

"Are you with the lumber company?"

"No. I'm not with anybody."

"Are you lying?"

"No. I'm not lying."

"How do I know you're not lying?"

"Why would I lie?" Mal answered. It was becoming hard and painful to hold onto the rope, and the bear was now foraging directly below the tree.

"That bear looks hungry," the voice said.

"I'm hungry too," said Mal.

"Well, I don't have any food for you."

"I have food in my pack. I'd rather share it with you than the bear."

There was a long silence. After what seemed like several minutes, the spotlight flashed back on.

"If you can make it up here, you can eat up here," the voice said.

"Sounds better than *being* eaten down there."

Slowly, laboriously, painfully, Mal climbed up the rope using the redwood's bark as a foothold, grabbing onto stubs and branches to rest whenever he could. From where he started above the bear, Mal gradually climbed another one hundred and sixty feet up into the tree. Now, five feet above him, he could see where the voice was coming from. It was a small wooden platform, about six by eight feet, built into the branches of the tree. It was partially covered with a flimsy plastic tarp.

He carefully climbed the last few feet directly into the glare of the spotlight and dragged himself onto the platform. The spotlight clicked off, leaving only the glow of a small oil lantern. What he saw there was extraordinary.

The voice belonged to a young woman, a stunningly beautiful young woman. She looked to be in her late teens, but it was hard to tell in the dim light. She was slender and fine-featured with long tousled blond hair. Her eyes were a brilliant blue. Her expression was calm and serene, and she seemed to project an aura that was almost ethereal. She reminded Mal of an angel.

"Good evening," were her first words.

"A better evening than I thought it would be a few minutes ago," said Mal as he surveyed the tiny, cramped and cluttered space, littered with empty water bottles, dirty clothing, overflowing bags of trash, and an ugly metal toilet pot.

"You entertain much?" asked Mal.

"Funny," she replied, mildly amused by the off-beat question.

"Maybe if you added a media room or at least hooked up to cable more people would visit," said Mal.

"Maybe I should have left you down there with that bear."

"Aw, that bear'll be fine. It'll find something to eat besides me. I'll tell you though, I wouldn't want to be a polar bear right now. I was up there in Hudson Bay not too long ago, and it's a god-awful mess."

Mal opened his backpack and pulled out an apple, a bag of cashew nuts, some pumpernickel bread, a banana, a chunk of cheese, a bar of chocolate, and a bottle of orange juice. The young woman grew wide-eyed at the sight, betraying how hungry she actually was, but Mal didn't seem to notice.

"Those bears are skinnier than ever," Mal continued.

"I've never heard of skinny polar bears. What's the matter with them?"

"Not enough ice," said Mal.

"Polar bears don't eat ice."

"No, they don't eat ice. They eat *on* the ice...on the ice floes where they hunt seals by smelling them from a mile away and then slowly sneaking up to their breathing holes and waiting, sometimes for hours, for a seal to pop up. When it does, the bear grabs it and bites it and eats it, and then starts the routine all over again."

"Poor seals."

"No, it's poor polar bears," said Mal, "because these days the ice has started melting earlier than usual, by at least two weeks. When the ice melts, the seals split, so when the bears come out of their dens from their winter hibernation, starving from having fasted and losing three or four hundred pounds, there are fewer seals to hunt because there's less of an ice pack to hunt them on. If the polar bear has cubs and doesn't catch enough seals to fatten her up, she can't nurse her cubs. If she can't do that she abandons them."

"What happens to the cubs?"

"Usually, they starve to death," said Mal. "So you see for a polar bear fat is where it's at, but they've been getting skinnier every year, and the ice is melting earlier every year, and so it looks like just a matter of time before there are no more polar bears."

"Do you know what's making the ice melt sooner?" the young woman asked knowingly.

"Humans," answered Mal, "worst thing on earth since T-Rex."

A flash of lightning lit the sky and thunder roared in the distance as Mal gestured for his new acquaintance to help herself to more food. They ate in silence, savoring every bite, as rain began to fall.

The only shelter from bad weather was a green plastic tarp suspended by ropes above the platform. As a roof it was far from perfect, but better than nothing at all. The wind picked up with a sudden gust, and the rain began to fall hard. The full brunt of the thunderstorm was starting to hit.

"It's not the best night for an after dinner walk," said Mal, "so if I promise not to snore, can I crash up here?"

"Only if you tell me what you're really doing here."

"Well," said Mal slowly, weighing what he was going to say, "I haven't been around these parts for a couple hundred years, so I thought I'd just come by and see if this forest was even still here. And, by the way, what are *you* doing here?"

"I'm living in this tree to keep it from being cut down."

Mal rolled his eyes and sighed as if he'd heard something absurd, something that also confirmed his worst fears. He knew that "tree sitting" was a last resort in a forest marked for death. As a tactic he believed it was futile, a feeble hopeless attempt to resist unstoppable forces of destruction.

"So, you're some kind of nature girl on a solo mission to save a tree?"

The young woman glared at Mal, ignoring what she took as a wisecrack.

"Well, all I can say is good luck," said Mal, "but I don't think you have a prayer."

The rain was lashing the forest now. Wind gusts roared ferociously through the majestic trees. As he curled up on the drenched wooden platform and tried to go to sleep, there was little doubt in Mal's mind that he'd encountered a beautiful misguided fool. The determined young tree sitter climbed into her wet hammock, suspended from branches above. She felt almost certain she had rescued some kind of wacko.

2

The Law

THE SUN ROSE OVER THE REDWOOD FOREST, gradually spreading its warmth, evaporating the wisps of foggy mist that had drifted in from the coast. Mal and the young tree sitter were awakened not by the sun's light, but by the loud, shrill blare of a bullhorn siren.

The bullhorn was in the hands of the county sheriff, but he wasn't the only one making noise down below. About twenty anti-logging activists belonging to a group called Green Earth began chanting in unison.

"Save the redwoods! Save the planet! Green Earth! Green Earth!"

Roughly as many local lumbermen began taunting and cursing the activists, while several deputy sheriffs kept the two groups apart. Standing on the sidelines, a wide-eyed young cub reporter from the local paper hastily scribbled down notes.

The commotion was loud and clear, a hundred and eighty five feet above the forest floor.

"Why don't you filthy tree-huggers go get a job!" yelled a logger.

"Why don't you greedy tree-killers stop destroying our planet!" replied an activist.

The sheriff ordered both groups to quiet down, stared up at the platform high above him and raised the bullhorn up to his lips.

"You are hereby notified that by residing in this tree you are trespassing on private property," said the sheriff. "You are hereby served with an eviction notice and must vacate this tree and this property within forty-eight hours."

With that, a deputy sheriff placed the official eviction notice against the giant redwood and nailed it into the trunk.

Immediately, the activists resumed their chanting, "Save our forests...Save our planet," over and over again.

"Why don't you save your breath," a lumberjack yelled at the activists. Another lumberman smiled menacingly as he waved a 'good-bye' up at the platform.

"Alright, party's over," shouted the sheriff into his bullhorn. "Everybody, and I mean everybody, can go home now. You have two minutes to leave or you'll be arrested."

Careful not to be spotted, Mal watched from the platform as the crowd gradually calmed down. The lumbermen left first, satisfied for the moment with the sheriff's action. Soon, the protesters followed, making their way in small groups down the winding dirt logging road that led out of the forest.

"Forget about the media room," said Mal. "That may not be such a good idea anymore."

The beautiful young tree sitter simply stared at Mal in disbelief, while thinking the words 'wacko nut case.'

"What *is* a good idea," said Mal, "is for you to flee this tree before they come and arrest you. That guy in charge of the bullhorn sounded like he means business."

"I'm *not* leaving here. Look what they've already done."

She pointed to the east, where in the distance Mal could see the area where hundreds of the redwoods had been cut down by the lumber company, leaving the hillsides bare and disfigured from the logging technique called "clear cutting." It looked like a battlefield. She told him about the low grade napalm spread by helicopters to burn away the invading weeds and junky shrubs that grow back in place of the redwoods. She told him about the homes destroyed by landslides and floods because the soil can no longer retain water...about the rivers filled with silt preventing the salmon from spawning...about the polluting smoke belching from the chimneys of the lumber mill.

None of this was news to Mal.

"I know, I know, I know all about it," Mal said wearily. "It's humans showing off their human nature."

"But it doesn't have to be that way," Sophie responded. "If people knew what was happening here...I mean, someone has to take a stand and try to call attention to how wrong and destructive this is and try to bring a stop to it."

"Look," said Mal, "there's never been a tree sitter who ever saved a tree. It's a lost cause. Trees are on the way out. Look at history. This whole country used to be covered with forests, but now they're pretty well gone. It won't be long before the rainforests of the Amazon are wasted, not to mention Indonesia and a lot of other places where people like you are killed for sport.

Somewhere on earth, humans cut down a chunk of forest the size of a football field every second of every day. Soon the whole planet won't have any trees at all, just a lot of toothpicks and patio furniture."

"How do you know all this?"

"I've been there. I've seen it. You can't imagine the things I've seen," said Mal.

"Maybe not. But I'm staying here."

"Okay. Fine. It's your decision, but I'll be on my way. I do appreciate the hospitality. Jail's gonna be much more comfortable for you than this soggy piece of plywood."

Mal grabbed the climbing rope, dropped it toward the ground, and then began to lower himself down the redwood. He paused for a moment and looked back up at the platform.

"So, what's your name?" he asked.

"Sophie," she replied.

"Short for Sophia?"

"Yeah. What's Mal short for?"

"Malchus. That's what the Romans called me, but my Hebrew name is Malachi. It means messenger."

'Malachi Malchus Shmalchus,' Sophie thought to herself as she took a last look at her uninvited guest, unsure of what to make of him.

Mal was glad to be leaving. He could smell trouble on the way, and trouble was something he'd learned to avoid long ago. His instincts told him to move on fast, but as Mal descended the huge gnarled trunk, he couldn't resist taking time to observe the wonders all around him.

He stopped to rest on a thick jutting branch high in the redwood's lush canopy. A few feet away, a rare spotted owl stared him in the face. Just below a gold and brown salamander, who lives its whole life in this giant tree, snapped up a gnat in its mouth.

On another branch, there were hanging gardens of ferns and thickets of huckleberries growing in layers of soil that had accumulated on the tree's wide limbs over the centuries. There were tiny pink earthworms in the soil and aquatic crustaceans called "copepods" living amid the ferns. How they got there was a mystery.

When he climbed a little farther down, Mal saw a baby eagle sitting quietly in its nest. He noticed a cluster of tiny edible mushrooms growing in the shade of another branch, but he didn't stop to eat them. Nearby, a perfect bonsai tree, which looked like a miniature oak, grew from a dirt-filled crack on a long, swaying foot-thick limb.

Mal knew that this ancient redwood was part of a special realm, a self-sustaining forest world that first arose in the age of the dinosaurs. As he continued the long climb down, Mal soaked up every detail. He sensed this might be his last look at a redwood, his last time to see one before they were wiped off the face of the earth.

When his feet finally touched the ground, Mal gazed back up at the towering tree and at Sophie's tiny platform high above. He couldn't see Sophie, but he noticed an osprey soaring in the sky. He knew they nested in the redwoods. He also knew that redwood trees supported the life of the forest, by providing not only shelter but a constant supply of fresh water.

As Mal began to walk away, a drop of water struck his cheek. He knew the water had started as fog earlier that morning. The redwood had captured the fog on its needles, where it condensed and then fell as a part of the five hundred gallons of moisture the tree gave the forest each day. Mal wiped the drop off with his forefinger, and tasted it on his tongue.

He also took a whiff of the air and savored its lemony fragrance. He loved the aroma of the redwood forest, unique in all the world, but he didn't know where it came from. Did it come just from the ancient living trees or also from their fallen dead leaves being decomposed by fungi, banana slugs and redwood snails? Or maybe it came from "nurse logs," like the one he was walking past.

Mal knew when a redwood succumbed to old age, often after two thousand years, it began a new life as a log for as long as five more centuries. The downed tree provided homes for numerous creatures such as chipmunks, voles and squirrels. Its bark became a perfect place for insects like crickets and beetles to lay their eggs. As the dead nurse log slowly decayed, the wood became a spongy wet reservoir, releasing water through the dry summer. Plants took root and grew on the log as it gradually disintegrated and fed the soil with its nutrients, which helped other trees to grow.

As he ducked under the giant sword fern that stood by the fallen redwood, Mal guessed that the smell of the forest arose from a subtle mixture of things, like a fine and rare perfume.

Bright red spots of color caught the corner of Mal's eye, and as he turned to see more closely, a smile spread over his face. It was the smile of a hungry man who'd seen a neon sign reading FOOD. It was a large wild gooseberry bush, dripping with fruit. Mal was there in an instant, devouring the ripe delicious feast the forest had provided.

Suddenly, behind him, Mal heard a loud whoosh. His nostrils burned as he spun around into a cloud of pepper spray.

"Freeze! You're under arrest."

"For what?" demanded Mal as he rubbed his eyes, now stinging and watering.

"You're on private property. You're trespassing. That's against the law," snarled the huge, towering, monster of a man as he pointed a king-size pepper spray canister at Mal's face. The man was at least six-foot-six and built like a gorilla. He was dressed in jeans and an official-looking khaki shirt with epaulets on the shoulders. He wasn't wearing a badge, but sewn above his shirt pocket was a black and white embroidered patch that read SECURITY.

Mal was fuming mad at being ambushed from behind, but when Mal got angry at someone he never cursed. He preferred the Shakespearean insult.

"Thou gleeking, hedge-born, clotpole, why'd you spray me with that stuff? You could just ask me to leave."

"You crazy hippy tree-huggers are causing a lot of trouble around here, and it's comin' to a stop."

Mal stood up out of his crouch, still rubbing his eyes, and then squinted intently at the man's right shoulder.

"An errant plop hath fouled thy frock," said Mal.

"What'd you say to me, tree-hugger?" the big man threatened.

"A bird pooped on your shirt," said Mal.

The man looked down, and Mal was off, running full-speed through the forest. It was the oldest trick in the book, and Mal could hear the man in pursuit.

"Whoooooooshhh." The pepper spray can fired again, but Mal was running into the wind and the burning mist never reached him. Mal leaped over a small nurse log, turned sharp behind a jagged stump, then zigzagged quickly through a dense, shady stand of young trees. Still moving as fast as he could, he dashed through a huge patch of ferns, jumped a salmonberry bramble, hopped through a thicket of currants, and then finally stopped, exhausted and lost at the base of a massive tree.

He gasped to catch his breath, when the end of a long red climbing rope bopped him on the head. Now, Mal knew where he was.

3

The Higher Law

MAL COULD SEE NO SIGN OF THE HULKING security man who was after him, but felt sure he was still around. Winded, Mal looked up the tree, not eager to perform once more the one hundred and eighty something foot climb, but he knew he had no choice. Using every last bit of his strength and energy, he slowly grappled his way back up to Sophie's platform.

"Good morning," were her first words.

"No, bad morning," said Mal. "Who is that huge surly guy who likes to blast people with pepper spray?"

"Oh, that had to be the chief of the private security goons hired by the lumber company," Sophie replied. "We call him Bigfoot."

"I'll tell ya, I haven't run that hard since the Huns were after me. Now those guys were goons, real brutes. Ugly to a man, and absolutely no sense of humor. They didn't have pepper spray though. They had spears and swords and bows and arrows, and they loved to use them."

Sophie simply stared at Mal.

"Now, make no mistake, the Romans were a real pain, but at least they played by the rules. They had laws and they followed orders, but the Huns were out of control. Vicious, nasty little dudes who did whatever they felt like."

"Who *are* you?" asked Sophie.

"Who are *you*?" replied Mal.

"I'm someone who's trying to make a difference, who's trying to save something ancient and beautiful."

"Good for you," said Mal. "But better still is for us both to sneak out of here as soon as possible. Probably smart to do it at night."

"I've told you already, I'm not leaving. I'm staying and I'm saving this tree."

"Hey, that's cool, but you're way too late. Until a couple of centuries ago, this was the most perfect forest on the planet. Some Indians were here and they lived off the land, and then the white man came. They came with saws and they started cutting, selling wood to make money. The work was hard and slow, and they didn't do much damage, but then some guy invented power tools. They called it 'progress' and they thought they were smart because now it was easier to cut trees down. As the power tools got more powerful, more redwoods got cut down. Then some genius got the idea of cutting *all* the trees down as a way to make lots of money to buy bigger and better things. He figured the trees were worth more as wood than as an ancient living forest. That's why there's just a tiny sliver of redwood forest left today. It's the law of supply and demand."

"I know about the history of the redwoods," said Sophie, "and I also know there's a higher law that says some things are just more important and more valuable than money. And I know that this forest wasn't created in order to be destroyed."

"So do you belong to some Druid cult that believes in nature worship?" Mal asked with a tease in his voice. "Or maybe you're some kind of New Age environmental born-again save-the-world Jesus freak."

"I don't belong to a Druid cult, and I'm not any kind of freak, and what have you got against Jesus?" asked Sophie.

"Nothing, but after I met him my life was never the same."

A sharp whistle pierced the stillness of the forest. The whoosh of a pepper spray canister sounded a second later. Both Mal and Sophie popped their heads out over the edge of the platform and surveyed the forest floor below. Bigfoot was back, chasing a Green Earth activist. "You're trespassing!" Bigfoot barked as he strained to run down a much younger man who taunted him as fled: "You're too feeble to catch me, you fat lumbering ape!" Mal could see that Bigfoot had little chance of catching his quick, nimble prey. "Whooooosh." The pepper spray fired off once again as the chase disappeared from view.

Now, someone whistled again, and Sophie grabbed a thin, coiled rope with a hook that snaps shut called a "karabiner" attached to the end. As she tossed it down toward the ground, another Green Earth guy appeared, running full speed toward the tree with a nylon bag in his arms. He snapped the bag onto the karabiner, performed a brief medley of loud gorilla howls and chimpanzee shrieks, and ran back into the forest.

"Give me a hand. Please!" Sophie pleaded as she pulled furiously on the rope, struggling to lift the weight now attached to it. Mal reached over and helped her haul up the bag.

"That was a clever strategy down there," said Mal as he tugged away.

"Diversionary tactics. It's the only way to get supplies past the security goons."

"Diversions are tricky. I've had 'em backfire," said Mal.

When the bag was in reach, Sophie grabbed it, unhooked it, and rushed to examine its contents. Two five-gallon plastic jugs of water accounted for the weight. The only other thing inside was a box of instant oatmeal. Sophie looked disappointed. She was hoping for more food.

Sophie poured some of the water into a banged-up metal pot, then lit her tiny camping burner. She hoped there was enough fuel left to get the water boiling, so at least the oatmeal could be cooked.

"If you can spare some oatmeal, this'll be my last supper here," said Mal. "I'm gonna beat a retreat tonight, under cover of darkness, as they say."

"I'm glad to share what I have, but tell me something," said Sophie, as she began preparing their meal. "What did you mean about Jesus changing your life?"

"Oh, that's a long story, over two thousand years long."

"You expect me to believe that you met Jesus?" asked Sophie.

"I was younger than I am now. It was the spring of 33, a nice sunny day, with a light breeze blowing through Jerusalem. I was working in my sandal shop finishing up a very cool pair for this Roman official who had flat feet. Then I heard all this commotion coming from up the street. I stuck my head out the door, and I saw this God-awful scene. Roman soldiers with whips and spears, angry Israelites shaking their fists, women screaming, people jeering, dogs barking, everybody yelling at each other. And in the middle of it all was Jesus.

I'd heard of him and seen him around, and now he was being forced down my narrow little street surrounded by this wild mob. The soldiers were whipping and prodding Jesus, trying to make him go faster. This horrified woman at the front of the crowd rushed up to me in a panic and whispered, 'They're going to crucify Jesus!' Then a Roman soldier yelled at me, 'Hey, Jew cobbler, get out of the way!' I stepped back into my doorway, as part of the crowd pushed by, and then right in front of me, Jesus stopped to rest. He looked terrible, all bloody and exhausted, suffering horribly. I felt awful for him. This soldier was about to use his whip to get Jesus moving, so I tried to distract him with a joke and buy Jesus some time. I yelled, 'Hey, brave Roman, if you bought that Jesus a pair of my sandals he could walk faster.'

The Roman glared at me for a second and swung his whip anyway. Jesus winced from the pain of the lash to his back, and then he slowly turned his head and looked at me. And then, he spoke to me. He said, 'You shall walk the earth until the world ends.'

Then the Roman spoke to me in this sneering, mocking tone. He said, 'It sounds like your friend Jesus has put a curse on you.' Then he laughed. 'A curse?,' I thought to myself, 'I don't deserve a curse.' I was just trying to help a little, but everyone took offense."

Sophie stared at Mal blankly, a spoonful of hot oatmeal frozen in her hand. She blinked a few times, before she spoke.

"If I'm to believe your story, at least you tried to make a difference. You tried, in your own goofy way, to make a bad situation better," said Sophie.

"Yeah, but it didn't work. I was trying to be ironic, and nobody understood."

Sophie plopped three dollops of the oatmeal dinner onto a bent metal plate and handed it to Mal.

"So, what have you been doing since you met Jesus?" she asked skeptically.

"I've been walking the earth," said Mal. "I've been everywhere. Some people call me 'the Wandering Jew.'"

"Isn't that a fairy tale?"

"Not to me," answered Mal.

"So, how do you survive?" asked Sophie.

"Just like this. I tell stories of what I've seen and where I've been and what I know in exchange for a little food and a place to sleep. It's been a long time on the road, and I've lived a lot of lifetimes, but I'm pretty sure my wandering days are coming to an end."

Sophie didn't say a word as she set down her empty plate and stared out into the forest, wondering why fate had burdened her with this apparent lunatic.

"I think I need some space," she said. "I'm going to climb up into the crown...and meditate."

"You'll have plenty of time to meditate when you're sitting in a jail cell," said Mal.

Sophie ignored the remark and headed up toward her favorite place, a small cave burned out of the redwood's thick trunk by a lightning strike many years before. She loved to curl up inside it and feel like she was actually part of the tree.

As Sophie left the platform, Mal rolled onto his stomach to peer at the forest floor. He began to devise a strategy for his potentially risky night time escape.

4

The Darkness

AFTER THE SUN HAD SET, SOPHIE CRAWLED out of her special perch and began the tough climb down to the platform, nearly a hundred feet below. Between the limbs she looked out and saw both what she loved and what she hated, the good and the bad, the glorious and the despicable. In one direction was the thriving ancient forest, and in the other, the scarred, scorched, desolate earth that resulted from clear cutting redwood trees. Seeing what she hated only strengthened her resolve to protect what was left of what she loved.

As Sophie stepped back onto the platform, Mal noticed the sad expression on her face.

"Did you figure out how to save this tree, not to mention the rest of the forest?" he asked.

"Don't worry. I know what I'm doing. It's just depressing to see the clear cut in the red sunset light. It looks like a bomb hit it."

"A bomb did hit it," said Mal. "The consumption bomb. It's a big part of the arsenal in the human war on nature. The war's been escalating year after year, and now humans are devouring resources much faster than earth can replace them. Their appetite for things like wood, oil and coal is beyond what nature can re-supply. If everyone in the world lived like humans do here, you'd need four extra planets to keep up with demand.

It's only a matter of time before all the destruction backfires and explodes in the face of the whole human race. That'll be the day. I can see it coming. In fact, I saw a sign of it coming not too long ago. It's a brand new bomb called 'MOAB' -- 'the Mother Of All Bombs,' built to destroy Mother Nature."

Sophie had a sense that Mal was winding up for another one of his rants, and she was right.

"Don't be depressed about the redwoods," said Mal. "Go to Appalachia, where they're not just cutting down trees but blowing up whole mountains. Coal companies are doing what they call 'mountain top removal mining.' It's diabolical. They start by blasting the top of a mountain with dynamite. Then, giant machines drag the dirt away and dump it into the valleys, burying streams and rivers and poisoning fish and wildlife. Even larger machines then mine the coal, and trucks haul it away to power stations. There the coal's burned to make electricity, but the smoke from the burning coal billows into the air, polluting the atmosphere.

When they're done with one mountain, they move on to the next, leaving behind a bald plateau and a ruined, poisoned environment. The folks who live there fret and complain that they're losing their mountains and culture and heritage and identity. They've even got big-time lawyers fighting for their cause, but they can't stop the destruction.

And, here's one I'll never forget, and it's absolutely true. I met this scientist out there, who'd discovered a new species of fish in one of the Appalachian rivers. On the very day he discovered it, a batch of dumped chemicals flowing downriver made the species extinct."

"That's worse than your polar bear story," said Sophie.

"Well, the polar bear's part of the story, 'cause the smoke from coal to make electricity contributes to global warming, which is making the arctic ice melt. So whenever you leave on a light somewhere, you're making life dimmer for a polar bear."

It was dark now, not even moonlight, field conditions Mal considered perfect for his escape from the forest to somewhere less embattled.

Mal heard faint rustling down below and assumed it was an animal. A few moments later, a shrill, painful, shrieking sound pierced the stillness of the forest.

"Geeeeeeeeeeeeeeeeeeeeeeeeeeeeeeeeeeeeeeeeeeee eeeeeeeeeee!"

"I hear a smoke alarm on steroids," said Mal.

"Yeah, it's a siren. They've done it before," said Sophie. "Eventually the battery'll run out of power. They're just trying to irritate me and keep me from sleeping. They're trying to break my will, but it doesn't work."

"Geeeeeeeeeeeeeeeeeeeeeeeeeeeeeeeeeeeeeeeeeeee eeeeeeeeeee!"

"You're brave to refuse to surrender to psychological warfare," said Mal. "Actually, sleep deprivation is a basic form of torture."

"Well, I'm not giving in. Surrender isn't an option. I'm staying right here in this tree for as long as I can hold out."

"Fine," said Mal, "but as soon as I'm sure there's no one still down there, I'm afraid I'm going to desert you in the face of looming battle. You ever hear the old saying that 'discretion is the better part of valor?' If you're smart, and you are, you'll retreat and regroup to fight another day.

There's no way you're going to win this war. You're outnumbered and outgunned, and it's just a matter of time before you're out of this tree. In the meantime, I'm sticking my fingers in my ears. That siren is making me crazy."

"Geeeeeeeeeeeeeeeeeeeeeeeeeeeeeeeeeeeeeeeeeee eeeeeeeeee!"

Sophie didn't even try to respond. It was too hard to talk with the siren blaring. She pulled two balls of cotton from her pocket and stuffed them into her ears.

The two sat silently on the platform, leaning against the tree, watching the changing night sky, the stars, the slow rotation of the heavens as the earth spun, all the while trying to ignore the siren, pretending the screeching wasn't slowly driving them nuts.

After more than seven hours, the siren petered out, its battery exhausted. Both Mal and Sophie were also exhausted.

It was three o'clock in the morning, and neither had gotten any sleep.

"Thank God that's over," said Mal. "That siren was evil."

"You get used to it," said Sophie.

"I guess you have to. And I guess I have to give up on trying to get you to abandon this soggy little platform with a view. So it's time, once more, for me to flee…"

The sound of breaking glass interrupted Mal. Both he and Sophie instantly peered down into the darkness below. They couldn't see a thing, but now they heard laughter. Men's laughter. It was the kind of loud, giddy, exaggerated laughter often heard when people were drunk and laughing at something that wasn't really funny.

"Whoever that is, they're certainly not sneaking around," said Mal.

Now they heard footsteps getting closer, mumbling, and then a "click." Next came the "pop" and the "zing."

"That was a bullet," whispered Mal. "A low caliber bullet, probably a twenty-two."

"Pop-Zing" once again, followed by more laughter out of the dark.

"They're shooting at us!" whispered Sophie, who was frozen, like Mal, on hands and knees, listening.

"WhaaaaaaaaaaaaWhoooooooooooo!" echoed up through the forest. Then a brief cackle of a laugh.

"Pop-Zing-Whing." This time, a bullet ricocheted very close by. Mal and Sophie stayed motionless on the platform.

Only silence now. Nothing. Then they heard a sound like someone falling into a bush. A short grunt, a low moan, vegetation rustling, another cackling laugh, and then stumbling footsteps gradually fading away.

"Not a textbook surprise attack, but those bullets were real," said Mal.

"That was kinda scary," said Sophie, "but I'm not gonna be scared away by some drunken security goons or out-of-work lumbermen or whoever those idiots were."

"So, you're willing to die for a tree?" asked Mal.

"If I weren't here, this tree would be dead," said Sophie.

"With or without you, there's not a chance this tree will die of old age," said Mal. "And speaking of chances, in case those trigger-happy party animals are still lurking down there, I think I'll wait for the dawn's early light to get on my merry way."

"Fine." said Sophie.

Sophie was more frightened than she let on. She was tired and hungry and struggling to keep a brave face. The bullets had rattled her. She realized how easily she could have just been killed.

5

The Light

THE SUN HADN'T RISEN YET, BUT THE predawn light made the fog visible in the sky. Mal stuffed his coat into his backpack and was almost ready to begin the climb down. The same sharp whistle heard the day before pierced the forest again. Though she'd had no sleep, Sophie snapped to attention and reached reflexively for the skinny rope with the karabiner attached. Hunger had a way of concentrating her mind. Both Sophie and Mal poked their heads over the platform and searched the ground for a sign of someone from the Green Earth supply line team.

The supply guy who'd run for it yesterday had obviously escaped Bigfoot and his pepper spray because he suddenly reappeared from nowhere at the base of the tree. He scanned the area nervously and then looked up at the platform. He whistled again, and Sophie began to lower the rope. Out of a pocket of ground fog appeared the second supply guy, clutching a nylon sack, and running hard for the tree. Suddenly clouds of pepper spray blasted in from every direction. Four big security men wearing gas masks charged the stunned supply guys and tackled them to the ground.

"Holy Moses," Mal muttered to himself. Sophie quickly pulled the slack rope back up.

The supply guys offered no resistance. The ambush had taken them by surprise, and overwhelmed them with superior force. Being totally passive now was part of their own strategy, part of their code of non-violence. The security men kept them pinned face down on the ground, and "zip-tied" their arms behind their backs with thick white plastic strips that ratcheted tight in one direction and would have to be cut to be removed.

With their enemy captured and under control, the men removed their gas masks. The biggest and oldest was Bigfoot. He walked over to the nylon sack meant for Sophie. He kicked it lightly, then picked it up, opened it and looked inside. It was filled with food and a few other provisions such as toilet paper. Then he tilted his head back and stared up at the platform, smiling smugly.

"Forget about breakfast," said Mal.

"There's still some oatmeal left," said Sophie.

"Lucky for you," said Mal. "The smell of pepper spray ruined my appetite."

Bigfoot tossed the supply sack aside and walked over to his prisoners. Each had a boot pressed onto their back compliments of two of the other security guys who were young and strong with tough looks on their faces.

"Alright, you two, get up," said Bigfoot, as the security men removed their feet. Mal and Sophie could hear it all clearly in the now quiet forest.

"We're not moving," answered one of the supply guys, the one that Bigfoot had chased before.

"Oh, you're gonna move, one way or the other," said Bigfoot.

Mal noticed two uniformed county sheriff officers walking toward the scene below. Bigfoot noticed them too, nodded recognition, and said nothing more as they approached.

"Whadda we got here?" asked one of the deputy sheriffs.

"Two trespassers who refuse to leave," said Bigfoot. "I believe they may be planning a tree-hugger sit-down strike."

"We would if we were sitting," said one of the supply guys, still face down on the ground.

"All right. You are both under arrest for trespassing," said one of the sheriffs. "If you refuse to move voluntarily, you'll be forcibly removed."

"Yeah, and that'll allow these guys to remove the whole forest," replied the supply guy.

From the platform, Mal and Sophie watched as the sheriffs tried to force the supply guys to stand up and walk. When they were lifted up onto their feet, they refused to stand and slumped back down. It was a technique called "passive resistance." Frustrated after several attempts at lifting, the sheriffs pulled out their own pepper spray. With the supply guys still "zip-tied" and now sitting on the ground, they methodically shot the pepper spray directly into their eyes from about an inch away. It was a technically legal technique called "pain-compliance" and had been used by the county sheriffs on uncooperative protesters in the past. The supply guys screamed in pain at the agonizing, burning sting in their eyes. Then the sheriffs told Bigfoot's boys to pick them up and carry them away.

Now both of the sheriffs turned their attention to Sophie's tree.

One of them scanned the eviction notice still nailed to the trunk. He then looked up at the platform, placed his hands around his mouth to form a megaphone, and issued an official warning:

"You've now got twenty-four hours to get out of here," he shouted.

The sheriffs walked away, and Sophie stared out at the neighboring trees, a pained expression on her face as she pondered what had befallen the supply guys.

"How did you get mixed up with these 'tree-huggers'?" asked Mal.

"My boyfriend was a member of Green Earth. He got me involved. He taught me the importance of doing positive things and trying to make a difference in the world. He also got me reading people like Thoreau who said that nature was the salvation of the world."

"You a drop-out?"

"Kind of. At the moment," said Sophie. "At school I felt like I was being programmed, to behave like some kind of social insect, in a world I didn't want to be part of. I just got sick of the whole stupid scene. The nasty gossip, the cliques, the silly status symbol competition, the mindless partying. It all stopped feeling real. It started to seem superficial and empty. I couldn't stand it anymore."

"Are your parents tree-huggers?" asked Mal.

"Are you kidding? Ever heard of Relax?"

"You think I'm too wound up?" replied Mal.

"Yeah. But my stepfather makes a fortune with it. It's a laxative. They're even selling it in eastern Europe now. The salesmen are mainly former members of the secret police."

"I'll bet they're very persuasive," said Mal.

"My parents don't care about anything like trees. Just themselves. And their possessions. And working out," said Sophie.

"Well, they won't need Relax when they find out you're in jail," said Mal.

"They also hated my boyfriend," Sophie continued. "They thought he was a bad influence, a dirty, grungy eco-freak who'd get me into trouble."

"I think you're in trouble now," said Mal, "so where's your boyfriend when you need him?"

"He's dead. He died in the hospital two days after he fell. He was sitting that tree right next to us. He lost his grip on the traverse lines between our trees. He was trying to bring me some food."

"When did this happen?" asked Mal.

"Forty days ago today. We'd been sitting our trees for twenty-one days before that. The security goons cut off our supply line. We were getting desperate."

"He died, and you're still here?" asked Mal.

"We had a pact that whatever happened we wouldn't abandon our trees."

Mal was stunned into silence. He looked down from the platform. What he saw put a knot in his guts. Bigfoot and his boys were back, along with two lumberjacks carrying giant chainsaws.

"Holy guacamole," said Mal to himself.

Sophie took a look too.

"The security goons are there to make sure nobody tries to stop the cutting," said Sophie.

"So, how do you stop a chainsaw?" asked Mal.

"We've tried talking to the loggers, and we've chained ourselves together around the trunks of trees, but none of that has worked out very well.

They just ignore us or use brute force to get us out of their way. Actually sitting in trees, becoming part of them, is the only thing that's worked for any amount of time."

"You've got maybe another day left," said Mal.

Sophie reached for one of the plastic jugs of water, twisted off the plastic cap, and took a long thirsty slug.

"That'll be like gold real soon," said Mal.

"I've got enough to last me," said Sophie.

"Maybe you do, but a lot of earthlings don't or won't. Just like gold, there's only so much around, and if humans aren't wasting it they're polluting it and then always thirsting for more.

That plastic cap, though, will still be around when the last of the water wars are waged by the last of the humans for the last few drops of pure, fresh water left on earth. And that plastic cap will still be around when the very last human has died of thirst."

"Are you upset because the security goons came back?" asked Sophie, sensing that Mal was frustrated at not being able to leave and once again launching into one of his rants as a way to ventilate.

"I was upset when I saw a swirling galaxy of plastic trash twice the size of Texas floating in the middle of the Pacific Ocean. I saw armadas of plastic caps, fleets of plastic bags, flotillas of plastic bottles, six-pack rings, cigarette lighters, syringes, spray can nozzles, traffic cones, you name it, ugly plastic debris, disgusting flotsam and jetsam as far as the eye can see, drifting in a slow spiral a thousand miles from nowhere."

"How did all that garbage get there?" asked Sophie.

"Some of it's from ships, but most of it comes from land. It's blown or washed to sea, where it's not biodegradable. So, it'll last for centuries. Sea turtles mistake floating plastic bags for jellyfish, and choke when they try to eat them. Albatross think the plastic is food and feed it to their chicks, who die soon after their meal.

Coral reefs are dying too because the air and the water's heating up, thanks to global warming. And the sea level's rising, sinking islands that once were paradise. On Tuvalu in Polynesia, they've got cars and buses stacked on the beach to keep the surf from flooding houses and washing the island away.

And the oceans themselves are starting to die. 'Dead Zones' are forming all over. Humans have flushed so many chemicals and fertilizers and forms of pollution into the water that only primitive life can thrive.

Sharks are an endangered species. Whales and dolphins don't have a prayer. The highest forms of life are struggling for survival, trying to keep from being poisoned or hunted out of existence. Bacteria and algae, that's the future. The ocean's becoming a sea of primal slime."

Sophie simply stared at Mal and mentally braced herself, uncertain if his rant was over or if there was more to come. It wasn't over yet.

"I've traveled all over five continents and sailed the Seven Seas, and in all the time I've been here I've never seen things worse. The world's gone out of balance. Humans in just the last hundred years have trashed a beautiful planet. Life is on the brink in this so-called modern age. God knows how much longer anything will survive."

"If you're so concerned and upset," said Sophie very calmly, "why aren't you doing anything to make things better?"

The loud rasp of a chainsaw firing up shattered the serenity of the forest. Mal and Sophie looked down to see a lumberman begin slicing into the trunk of a redwood about fifty feet away. It was a younger, smaller tree than Sophie's, but it was still a terrible, painful sight for her to see.

"Rrrrrrrrrrrrrraaaaaaaaaaaaaaaaaaaaaaaaaaaa aaaahhhhhhhhh."

The lumberman attacked the tree with practiced skill and precision. The blaring noise of the chain-saw ripping through the bark and wood reverberated through the forest as he executed the initial cuts and then stopped to reposition.

"That logger is killing a living thing," said Sophie.

"Behold the mighty hand of progress," said Mal, mimicking the pompous "Voice of God" tone of a documentary film narrator.

"You're probably the most cynical, sarcastic person I've ever met," said Sophie.

"You've only been on earth a short time," said Mal.

"So was your friend Jesus," said Sophie, "and he was just one person who stood up for what he believed and changed the world."

"Yeah, but look what they did to him," said Mal.

"Rrrrrrrrrrrrrraaaaaaaaaaaaaaaaaaaaaaaaaaaa aaaahhhhhhhhh."

The deafening sound of the chainsaw was back, as the logger resumed his assault, cutting ever deeper into the tree.

"Someday there'll be a law against cutting down redwoods," said Sophie.

"It may not be a crime these days," said Mal, "but it sure seems like a sin."

"I can't watch this anymore," said Sophie. Mal didn't say a word, but he too looked away, out at the remaining trees.

After about a minute, the ear-splitting din halted, replaced by the less irritating rattle of the idling chainsaw engine. Then came the sharp cracking sound of wood splintering, which was quickly overwhelmed by the long, loud groan of the entire tree succumbing to the power of gravity. Seconds later, a thundering explosion, as the once mighty redwood smashed into the earth.

6

The Fallen

THE DUST CREATED BY THE FALLEN REDWOOD still swirled in the air as Mal and Sophie peered over the edge of the platform to witness the destruction below. The lumbermen were taking a break, sitting on tree stumps, assessing their conquest. The security detail was still on duty, on guard and ready for any insurgent Green Earth protesters who might have infiltrated the forest to disrupt or prevent the logging.

"Chalk up one more for the humans in the war on Mother Earth," said Mal. "There's yet another battle casualty dead on the ground below."

"The sound of a tree being killed is awful," said Sophie. "It sounds like they're committing this slow, brutal, agonizing premeditated murder on a completely helpless, defenseless victim."

"Those lumberjacks aren't exactly depraved war criminals," said Mal. "They're just humans following orders in order to make a living. It's worse to hear a glacier dying. There's no sawing or cracking, no moaning and groaning, just a steady drip, drip, drip, like ancient Chinese water torture."

"I know there are other problems in the world. I know that glaciers are shrinking."

"A lot faster than the Holy Roman Empire did," said Mal. "They're in full retreat all over the world. They're shrinking so fast that it's given the term 'glacial movement' new meaning. Soon Glacier National Park will have no glaciers, and the snows of Kilimanjaro will be history. That mountain's glacial snow and ice is melting so quickly that a scientist actually wanted to cover it with plastic to reflect heat and save the snow while they tried to figure out what the hell's going on. Same thing up in Alaska, and the Rockies and the Andes and Alps and the Himalayas.

Greenland's the scariest. The glaciers there are melting three times faster than anyone thought before. Science folks are freaking out because all that ice cold water could change ocean currents like the Gulf Stream and turn Europe into Siberia. And sea levels could rise as much as twenty feet, flooding the coastlines of the world and driving tens of millions of people inland to higher ground."

"Brrrrrrruuuuuuuunnnnnnnnggggggnnnnnggggnn nnggggnnnnn."

A chainsaw fired up below. Sophie closed her eyes. Mal looked over the platform. Another logger with a longer chainsaw had set his sights on a larger tree that was even closer to Sophie's giant. The trunk had been marked with spray paint, targeted for cutting.

Standing close beside the tree, the logger revved the saw's engine and pressed the sharp, spinning chain blades into the gnarled bark.

"Rrrrrrrrrrrrrrraaaaaaaaaaaaaaaaaaaaaaaaaaaaa aaaahhhhhhhhhh."

His first cut gashed a deep open wound, but the first wound was never fatal. Sophie couldn't stand to watch and stared off into the distance. This time Mal observed every detail, the notch cuts and back cuts, as the saw ripped through the living wood until the tree began to fall.

The cracking and the groaning was louder this time because the tree was larger and closer. For a moment Mal thought the tree was coming at them because of his perspective from high above. But it fell at a narrow angle to the platform and landed with the sound of a bomb going off.

The ground shuddered from the impact and sent tremors through the forest, shock waves so strong that Mal and Sophie literally felt the vibration high on their plywood perch.

"I guess that's a redwood's death rattle," said Mal.

"I feel sick," said Sophie. "This is so wrong, so stupid, so mindlessly..."

"BrrruunngguuunnngguuunnnRrrrrraaaaaaaaa aaaaaaaaahhh."

A third tree, even closer, was already being cut.

"They're right next to us," said Sophie as she looked down at the loggers and security men, some of whom were now looking up at her and the platform.

Then Sophie noticed something unusual. Everyone but the logger who was cutting the nearby tree began to walk away. Within a few moments they were all out of sight.

"Rrrrrrrrrrrrraaaaaaaaaaaaaaaaaaaaaaaaaaaa aaaahhhhhhhhh."

Mal looked down at the tree cutter, who was working hard and fast. Suddenly, the chainsaw stopped and the logger dashed away. There was only silence now. A few seconds later, the sound of wood cracking.

"I don't believe this," said Sophie, standing paralyzed at the edge of the platform.

Mal grabbed Sophie's arm and pulled her close to the trunk. Then came the groaning sound of the cut tree losing its strength and starting to fall. It was headed right for the platform.

"Holy Grail," said Mal as the giant trunk swung directly toward them, tearing off large branches above as it banged and skidded down the side of the tree, kicking off clouds of dirt and debris, sending sharp wood splinters flying, and shaking the tiny platform as if it were hit by a monster earthquake. The sound grew louder and more terrifying as the falling tree smashed closer and then in a blink swept past the platform, missing it by inches, before it struck the ground with a booming, shattering roar.

For what might have been a minute, Mal and Sophie stared at each other in shock, frozen in place on the platform, pressed against the trunk of the tree. Then Mal broke the silence.

"Now I'm mad," were his first words. "That was no accident. Those dudes can drop a tree on a dime. They did that deliberately. What do those humans think they're doing? They could have just killed you with that terror tactic."

"Not to mention you," said Sophie.

"For me it's not an issue," said Mal. "Wounds are what I worry about. I can't bear pain and suffering, especially when it's my own."

Sophie stared at Mal blankly in disbelief, still recovering from the trauma of what had just happened.

The forest was still again. A gentle breeze drifted through the trees. Birds chirped in the distance. The sun shined past scattered billowing clouds. Mal and Sophie stayed seated on the platform bracing their backs against the trunk of the tree and gazing out at the forest.

Mal wasn't given to soul-searching. He usually tried to avoid it by staying on the move. But as he stared at the giant redwoods and the beautiful clouds and the bright blue sky, he knew that something had gotten under his skin, something he couldn't put his finger on.

He knew that he was mad at the loggers for their dangerous, nearly deadly assault. He also knew he was mad at himself for not foreseeing the attack. And then there was Sophie. He knew he wasn't mad at Sophie, just frustrated by her foolish, stubborn naivety that didn't seem to comprehend the powerful, undefeatable forces being marshaled against her. At the same time, he couldn't help admiring her courage.

Experience had taught Mal that it was usually wise to retreat from conflict, to stay out of other people's battles, to avoid getting involved in struggles that weren't his own. His instincts had told him to leave the forest soon after he arrived. Yet there was something new now going on inside him. Something was churning and changing, and making him resist his usual survival strategy.

Mal thought of how Sophie had called him the most cynical and sarcastic person she'd ever met. He'd brushed off the remark with a wisecrack, but the description had hurt him in a way he couldn't define. It was more than a superficial flesh wound. The remark had penetrated deep into his soul, and led Mal to realize that Sophie reminded him of something. She reminded him of himself, of the way he used to be before he began to give up on the world.

An eagle flew past the tree, carrying food to her nesting chicks. In that moment, Mal experienced a revelation, an epiphany of a kind, a sudden flash of recognition that restored an abandoned belief, a belief in the power of one person to make a difference in the world.

Mal set his thoughts aside for a moment and tested Sophie's resolve.

"Now that you've caught your breath, isn't it time to give up this fight and climb down this tree while you still can, while you're still alive?" asked Mal.

"Now's a good time for *you* to leave," said Sophie. "It doesn't look like there's anyone down there, so this is your chance to escape."

"Maybe so, but I'm hearing this little voice in my head and it's telling me not to go," said Mal.

"The fact that you hear voices in your head doesn't completely surprise me. And another fact is that I'm not going down, in fact, I'm going up higher."

"You've got a special place up there in the canopy, a meditation room?" asked Mal.

"Something like that, but to me this whole forest is a special place, a sacred place, and my lightning cave up there is my little heaven on earth."

"You're full of little surprises," said Mal, "surprises that scare me to death. I've been getting this funny feeling that you're really, truly serious about trying to save this tree."

"You haven't believed me 'til now?" asked Sophie.

"Most folks give up in the face of danger. They surrender to fear and superior power. And I'll tell ya, in all the years I've been on earth I've seen lots of folks take on causes, good causes and bad causes, but not that many humans are ready to go the distance, to commit totally and completely, to sacrifice everything for what they believe in. When somebody's in that state of mind you've gotta respect it, and I've been starting to think that you may actually be somebody like that."

"People always said I was stubborn," said Sophie. "And I'm not giving up now after everything I've been through, even though I have to admit I've gotten kinda scared."

"Are you being stubborn because of your boyfriend? Feeling guilty because of what happened?" asked Mal.

"I know I feel I owe it to him to stay up here as long as I can, no matter what happens. But I also feel I owe it to the forest. Cutting these trees down is just so wrong. It's really an atrocity."

"It's not the first one in history," said Mal, "and I bet it won't be the last."

"But that doesn't mean people shouldn't try to stop it."

"I'll tell you something I've realized and try not to be shocked," said Mal. "I thought I learned my lesson a long, long time ago, but what those lumbermen nearly did to you not only got me mad, it got me thinking. Thinking about courage and commitment and taking a stand. You've taught me something I've forgotten. It's that sometimes you can't sit back and watch. Sometimes you have to go into action even when it seems futile."

Sophie didn't look shocked, only startled, as Mal continued.

"So what I'm saying is I'm not leaving. I'm volunteering to enlist in your crusade. We can't let those lumber guys get away with what they're doing, and I won't leave you alone up here. I can't desert you now. Besides, I feel I owe you for saving me from that bear."

7

The Climb

FOR THE FIRST TIME SINCE THE PLATFORM was nearly ripped to the ground, Sophie stood up, reached for a small branch above her, and began climbing up toward the lightning cave she loved.

"Mind if I tag along?" asked Mal.

"If you can make it, be my guest," answered Sophie.

The often fickle weather was still fairly warm and sunny as Sophie expertly ascended up toward the canopy using the tree's many smaller jutting branches as a natural spiral stairway. Mal followed a few feet behind, trying to copy Sophie's well-practiced moves. After a couple minutes, Sophie stopped to rest and survey the next leg of the climb.

Mal used the moment to ask about something on his mind.

"So, you don't think being cynical or sarcastic is funny, do you?"

"I think it's just a defense, and I don't believe that cynicism or sarcasm has ever changed anything for the better," said Sophie.

"You're a very serious person," said Mal.

"I'm serious about saving this tree," said Sophie as she pulled herself up to a higher branch.

Mal continued to follow in her footsteps, and then he noticed something strange. Two climbing ropes, one about four feet above the other, were stretched across to a neighboring tree about twenty yards away.

"What are those ropes for?" asked Mal.

"Traverse lines," said Sophie. "It's a way to get from tree to tree. My boyfriend fell off those lines trying to get here."

Mal didn't say a word.

Sophie continued climbing up toward a thick twisted branch and then stopped. When Mal arrived a minute later, Sophie was eating huckleberries that grew on a wild thicket in the sunlight atop the branch. Mal picked several berries and popped them into his mouth.

"You a vegetarian?" asked Mal.

"You have a problem with that?"

"No, but you remind me of a cattle slaughterer I ran into not too long ago," said Mal.

"Thanks a lot."

"Yeah, he was one tough Texas cowboy with an appetite for trouble, just like you. Or at least the people he tangled with treated him like a trouble-maker. Now this is a dude who loved to use his 'knocking gun.' That's a metal tube with a pistol cartridge that kills a cow by driving a bolt into its brain. He was a real pro, fast and efficient, and he knew how to get into the cattle's 'flight zones' when they got nervous and tried to escape.

He told me that killing was really fun, that it beat de-boning, which he thought of as girl's work. The trouble was that he slaughtered what the government claimed was the only cow ever found in the country with mad cow disease, which is pretty well sure to eventually kill the humans who eat the beef or burger that came from the sick cow.

The real trouble started a little bit later when he talked to reporters about killing that cow. He told them he was sure that the cow was ground-up into hamburger and had already been eaten. He said he thought that the records were forged to cover up that fact, that not enough cattle were ever tested to say that beef is safe, that regular slaughtering methods just weren't all that good for preventing the spread of mad cow disease."

"What happened to him?" asked Sophie.

"He got fired and harassed by the government, who wanted him to shut up and quit causing a ruckus."

"Cattle slaughtering sounds awful," said Sophie.

"Cattle raising is worse. Now there's another problem worth standing up against. Most folks have a picture of nursing calves with cows munching on grass and hay, but that's not what usually goes on. Now you've got these huge factory farms where calves are fed cow's blood instead of milk, and cows have to eat the ground-up remains of chickens and pigs that were fattened up on the ground-up brains and spines and bones of cows, which could bring mad cow disease full circle back to the cows and the humans who eat beef."

"It's like calves have been turned into vampires, and cows have been forced to be cannibals," said Sophie. "It just doesn't sound natural."

"If cows were meant to eat meat, they'd run as fast as wolves and also have sharp teeth," said Mal. "But it gets worse because cows are given growth hormones and antibiotics and appetite enhancers, and other stuff, and no one's really quite sure what that does to humans once they've eaten their steak or burger. Add some fries to that and its no wonder so many folks are fat."

Sophie picked another huckleberry and plopped it in her mouth. She savored its natural sweet taste, but was reminded of how hungry she actually felt. Mal's story about the cattle business had temporarily suppressed her appetite. She ate another few berries, and turned to Mal.

"I didn't know all that about cows, but it all makes sense." said Sophie. "I've always believed that if you turn against nature, nature will turn against you."

"It's more than a belief. It's a natural law."

Sophie said nothing and resumed the climb, slowly leading Mal another fifty feet up through redwood's vast, tangled canopy. Then just above them there appeared a small brightly lit area without shading foliage or branches.

There in the redwood's trunk was a gaping hole more than three feet wide at the bottom and gradually tapering up in the shape of a water drop. Decades perhaps centuries before, a lightning bolt struck the tree here and burned a small cave into its trunk. The tree withstood the assault and recovered from the wound and now it was a special part of its living, growing architecture.

For Sophie it was a magical roost, a place to commune with her tree and admire the surrounding forest, a place to be alone and at one with the natural world, a place to reflect or meditate or pray. She grabbed a small branch beside the cave and backed herself into her perch. She signaled to Mal to join her. There was just room enough for two to sit inside and gaze out across the forest while the late morning sunlight warmed them.

"Nice little spot in the sun," said Mal. "Good place to work on your tan."

"Up here I feel like I'm good friends with this tree and the forest and the sun," said Sophie.

"Well if you lived way down in South America instead of in this tree, the sun would be your enemy. Daylight there is dangerous now, and for a lot of folks it's deadly. On some days, you're supposed wear special sunglasses, cover your exposed skin with sun cream, wear long-sleeved shirts and wide-brimmed hats or use a sun umbrella. On other days nobody goes outside.

In this Chilean town called Punta Arenas, they've installed these little 'sun traffic lights' called 'solmaforos' that change color to tell you how bad things are. Skin cancer's going through the roof because by the time you're eighteen years old you've already been blasted by a lifetime's worth of sunlight."

"What are you talking about?" asked Sophie.

"I'm talking about a giant hole in the ozone that lets in too much ultraviolet light. When I was down there I got fried before I knew what hit me. Had a great tan though."

"So why is there a huge hole in the ozone?" asked Sophie.

"Humans. What else? See, the earth has a layer of ozone around it and the ozone reflects ultraviolet light. Too much ultraviolet radiation can cause skin cancer and even kill tiny plants in the food chain. The reason there's too much down there in Chile is because of the hole in the ozone layer in the sky above it. It's a big gaping hole, larger than the landmass of the United States. It was caused by man-made chemicals like refrigerator coolants and aerosol sprays that got into the atmosphere, drifted south, and then changed life on the earth below it. Whoever thought hairspray would come back to mess things up?"

Sophie stared up at the sky and didn't say a word. The forest was still, with not a modern man-made sound to be heard until a few moments later when far in the distance a faint unearthly thumping noise resembling rapid cannon fire broke the calm.

"Boofbooofboofboofboofboofboofboofboof boofboofboof."

"You hear that?" asked Mal.

"Of course I hear it."

"What is it?"

Sophie didn't answer, she just kept listening.

8

The Tempest

THE STRANGE RAPID THUMPING NOISE GREW louder and louder. Mal and Sophie now listened intently. It wasn't a pleasant sound to hear. It was ominous and foreboding.

"Boofbooofboofboofboofboofboofboofboof boofboofboofboofboof."

The distant steady ever-growing beat reverberated off the hillsides. Sophie scanned the sky, but could see nothing.

"Sounds like the beginning of Armageddon," said Mal. "Maybe the world's really coming to an end. Maybe I can quit wandering."

"I think I know what it is," said Sophie.

Suddenly, from down on the ground, rang other disturbing noises.

"BrrruunngguuunnngguuunnnRrrrrraaaa
aaaaaaaaaaaaaahhh."

The loggers were back. Lots of them. Also
Bigfoot and his boys. A second chainsaw fired up.
Then another. And another.

"Rrrrrrrrrrrrrraaaaaaaaaaaaaaaaaaaaaaaaaa
aaaahhhhhhhhh."

"Rrrrrrrrrrrrrraaaaaaaaaaaaaaaaaaaaaaaaaa
aaaahhhhhhhhh."

"Rrrrrrrrrrrrrraaaaaaaaaaaaaaaaaaaaaaaaaa
aaaaahhhhhhhhh."

The din of the chainsaws was overwhelming as
their sharp steel blades made fast work of cutting
away the branches from the trunks of the fallen
redwoods. Each of the trees was quickly being dis-
membered, their limbs systematically severed in
a shrieking deafening display of efficient, profes-
sional lumbering, executed with military precision.

"Rrrrrrrrrrrrrraaaaaaaaaaaaaaaaaaaaaaaaaa
aaaaahhhhhhhhh."

"BOOFBOOFBOOFBOOFBOOFBOOFBOOF
BOOFBOOFBOOF BOOF."

As if battling the screaming chainsaws, the
ungodly mechanical thumping noise pounded
even louder. Mal and Sophie clutched the sides
of the lightning cave as the frightening cacophony
escalated. A sudden quick blast of wind hit them
from above and swept past them like a cannon shot.

"I knew it. It's a helicopter. A logging helicopter,"
said Sophie.

"Choppers above and below," said Mal.

Sophie ignored the remark as she watched the huge roaring helicopter that had buzzed her tree from behind in the style of a sneak attack and could now be seen fairly high in the sky turning a wide circle back.

"It's getting dangerous up here," said Mal. "I feel like we're in a war zone."

Sophie said nothing. She grabbed a small branch and pulled herself out of the cave. She stood on another thicker branch just below its lip and stared up to the sky. Her favorite place in the tree had become a precarious perch. Still silent, she began the descent to the relative safety of the platform.

Mal quickly followed behind trying to mimic her climbing techniques. He had a hard time keeping pace as Sophie nimbly descended in circles on the natural ladder of jutting branches. The lumbermen below were still hard at work, hurriedly sawing off the last branches, their chainsaws screaming in unison.

The thundering beat of the helicopter grew louder again. Mal stopped climbing to take a look and felt a lump in his throat. What he saw was terrifying. The huge helicopter was close and hovering forward, descending directly for the tree.

"Stop climbing and get a grip!" Mal yelled down at Sophie.

A moment later it was upon them. The roar was almost unbearably loud as it inched just above the top of the tree and unleashed a powerful downdraft directly on Mal and Sophie. Each of them clung to branches with every ounce of their strength as the sudden raging gale force wind exploded against their bodies and tried to rip them to the ground.

The tempest stopped as quickly as it started when the helicopter hovered away, ascended into the sky, and began another wide arcing lap high above the trees. For a moment, Mal and Sophie stared at each other in shock. Mal took a slow deep breath as Sophie resumed the climb down. Off in the distance, the thumping engine could still be plainly heard. Down below, the chainsaws continued to shriek.

Just after they reached the platform, the logging helicopter arrived again, this time from the other side, but it stopped before reaching the tree. It hovered over the lumbermen and lowered a thick steel cable. Two of the lumbermen grabbed the cable and began to attach it to a fallen tree, which was now a huge branchless log.

From the platform, Mal and Sophie heard the roar of the helicopter's engine intensify. A tornado of sawdust and dirt swirled up from the ground as the giant log was lifted straight up toward the sky. With its roots sawed away, its branches cut off, suspended at one end by a steel line, the once majestic trunk slowly ascended and disappeared.

Both Mal and Sophie stayed silent for a long time, both gazing out across the forest, contemplating what had happened. Sophie was the first to speak.

"You know, I think living trees have souls that go to some kind of heaven when they die."

"Sounds better than the hell of the sawmill," said Mal.

Sophie stared out at the forest again. "The loggers have cut down nearly everything, and they still want the little bit that's left. They won't be satisfied until the redwoods are extinct."

"Hey, the giant redwoods aren't alone," said Mal. "Almost half the world's plants may face extinction, not to mention tigers, rhinos, gorillas, spotted owls, sea turtles. You know the depressing list. What's worse is that the science guys believe the world's on the verge of a mass extinction of wildlife. There've been five so far, and the last one took out the dinosaurs. How long do ya think a polar bear can tread water after the arctic ice melts?"

"I know about global warming," said Sophie.

"Unless folks get serious about trying to combat it, we can say our prayers now, and get ready for floods, famine, plagues, droughts, killer storms, and insect invasions. There'll be millions and millions of desperate humans wandering around looking for food and a safer place to live. We're in for a very long heat wave. It's a no-brainer. You fill the air with enough smoke and exhaust from burning oil and gas and coal, and it traps the heat like a greenhouse and starts to warm things up, and soon all hell breaks loose."

"Boofbooofboofboofboofboofboofboofboof boofboofboofboof."

The helicopter was on its way back to carry away another log. Its sound was no longer a mystery, but a thundering source of terror. Sophie looked nervous, but also focused and determined.

"It may seem like the world's being ruined," said Sophie, "but if people are brave and dedicated they can do something about their problems."

"I'm not sure what to do about that chopper. It's trying to blow us to kingdom come."

"BOOFBOOFBOOFBOOFBOOFBOOFBOOF BOOFBOOFBOOFBOOFBOOF."

The sound of the helicopter grew deafening as it swept in directly over the tree and blasted Mal and Sophie again with a sudden fierce shock of rotor wash. The helicopter now slowly descended straight down over the second huge log, and hovered in place as it lowered the steel cable. The loggers sprung into action, quickly attaching the cable to the giant hunk of now-dead wood. A brisk stream of air from the spinning blades whipped sideways at Mal and Sophie, pelting them with dirt and sawdust.

Sophie squinted, lowered her head, and tried to keep from inhaling any more of the cloud of flying debris. She coughed and cleared her throat.

"I'm starting to choke on this stuff," said Sophie.

"Well, at least it's organic," said Mal. "You wouldn't believe how much really bad stuff is blowing in the winds of the world. Now here's a cause worth fighting for. Take your average coal-burning power plant smokestack. It belches tons of carbon dioxide, which is the main cause of global warming, but also stuff like mercury, which falls back down to the ground and into lakes and rivers and streams.

I caught a fish in upstate New York and a park ranger told me not to eat it because it was full of mercury. He called it a 'consumption advisory.' Those smokestacks also pour out smog and other nasty particles, which give kids asthma and God knows what else just from breathing the air."

The helicopter's engine revved up and hurled more debris high into the air. Then the roaring, whirling "air crane," as it's called, rose slowly higher into the sky taking the redwood trunk with it. Mal and Sophie watched silently as the trunk passed not far from the platform. Another gust of rotor wash rushed past them as the helicopter headed for the sawmill.

"You know, I'll tell you something about the wind," said Mal. "It can airlift nasty stuff anywhere. When I was last up in Greenland, the local newspaper reported that the local native people, the Inuits, Greenland's Eskimos, had the highest human concentrations of industrial chemicals and pesticides of anyone on earth. Not only that, they tested some young Inuit mothers who were nursing their babies and found levels of chemicals so extreme that their breast milk would qualify as hazardous waste."

"That's unbelievable," said Sophie.

"It is until you think about it," said Mal. "It's like that fish full of mercury, but on a much bigger scale. See, northbound winds from America and Europe and Asia have been blowing pollution and chemicals up to the arctic for decades. They work their way into the food chain from fish to seals to whales, and that's what the Inuits eat. You'd think seal meat would be pure as driven snow but its full of hundreds of poisons like DDT and PCBs and PDPEs and, you guessed it, mercury."

"It's like they're lab rats for the world's pollution," said Sophie.

"Yeah, and meanwhile polar bears, full of the same pollutants, are drowning 'cause there's not enough ice, and unknown islands keep appearing out from under the melting glaciers," said Mal. "It won't be long before the North Pole is nothing but open water. So if the Inuits are lab rats for how much pollution humans can take, maybe everyone else is like frogs in a simmering cooking pot, who don't know the temperature's gradually rising up toward the boiling point."

"Boofbooofboofboofboofboofboofboofboof boofboofboof."

The helicopter was back again to pick up the last log. Mal and Sophie had almost gotten used to the deafening noise, the dust storms, and the sudden blasts of rotor wash. They watched the familiar routine of dropping the cable, attaching the log, and lifting it away.

Sophie's face bore a pained expression, and as the noise of the helicopter began to fade away, she turned to Mal and asked him a question.

"So tell me something," said Sophie, "I really appreciate that you want to help me, but do you ever *do* anything about the stuff that upsets you, or do you just like to rant and complain?"

"For a while, I thought it was futile because the world seemed totally doomed. It may well be, but I've realized that even when things seem hopeless, hope is the best thing we have. And the only way of fulfilling hope, if there's any chance, is by acting on what we hope for, in the face of any odds."

"Something's really come over you," said Sophie.

"Seems like you've inspired me," Mal replied.

"I think the only things worth fighting for are things much larger than yourself. Like these redwoods," said Sophie.

The sun was high in the sky now. On the forest floor below the loggers and security guards seemed to be taking a break. They were scattered around in the shade, a few munching a quick snack out of their metal lunch pails. Both Mal and Sophie were starving, but had nothing left to eat.

"I'm going to climb up higher and see if I can find some more berries," said Sophie.

"Boof booof boof boof boof boof boof boof boof boof boof boof boof."

The sound of the approaching helicopter stopped her in her tracks.

"Why's it coming back?" Sophie asked herself out loud, "It's taken all the logs away."

Mal peered over the edge of the platform to see if anything new was happening below. No one was there anymore, not the loggers or the guards. Mal looked up toward the sky and listened as the roar grew louder. Sophie did the same, and both sensed something was wrong.

"BOOFBOOFBOOFBOOFBOOFBOOFBOOF BOOF."

Suddenly, the helicopter appeared, flying low and slow and directly toward them. It stopped just above the top of the tree and hovered. In an instant the air-blast hit them, along with a hailing barrage of small branches, bark, and leaves, which exploded down like shrapnel.

Mal and Sophie tried to "duck and cover" against the violent onslaught. They hunched over close to the trunk, their hands cupped over their eyes in defense from the pounding storm of debris created by the man-made hurricane.

The plastic tarp ripped away, as Sophie's hammock spun in fast circles. Then her sleeping bag took flight along with her jacket, the lantern and lots of empty water bottles. Sawdust and dirt flew up from below, sucked into the powerful vortex created by the whirling blades of the log-ging helicopter.

The engine gunned louder, and Mal and Sophie were literally flattened by the ever more powerful, crushing torrent of air. They were slammed face-down upon the plywood platform, as it shook and struggled to survive the brutal airborne attack.

Pinned down by the bombardment, Mal and Sophie could do nothing. There was no way to resist the relentless, walloping tempest. They could only hope or pray the tiny platform would hold.

"I can't believe this is happening," murmured Sophie to herself.

"Trying to make a difference isn't always easy," said Mal.

What felt like an eternity really lasted only min-utes, until the helicopter began to ascend and quickly peeled away, its mission at least partly accomplished. Soon the forest was quiet again. Mal and Sophie had survived only because the plat-form had managed to cling to the tree.

9

The Climber

IT WAS STILL A BEAUTIFUL DAY, A SUNNY afternoon with a soft breeze blowing in from the west. Mal and Sophie remained sprawled face-down upon the battered platform, gradually recovering from the trauma the helicopter had inflicted. Mal slowly rolled over onto his back and sat up. He gazed across the forest, blinked his eyes, shook his head, and reflected on what had just happened.

"Now I'm *really* mad," were his first words. "Those chopper pilots are criminal. They're the ones who should be arrested...for assault with a deadly weapon."

Still prone on the plywood, Sophie turned her head to the side so she could speak.

"They'll say they didn't know anybody was in the tree. They'll say we were trespassing on private property, and didn't have a right to be here anyway."

"Doesn't the Bible say to forgive trespasses?" said Mal.

"Funny," said Sophie as the sound of rattling chains rang up from the forest floor. Mal and Sophie peered over the platform.

Below, a tall, powerfully-built logger wearing a plaid shirt, jeans, and a climbing harness was untangling a long steel chain. Climbing spikes were attached to his boots.

"Who is that dude?" asked Mal.

"Oh no, it's a climber," said Sophie. "What happens is the sheriff's department deputizes lumberjacks who're real good at climbing, and they send them up trees to bring tree sitters down. It's happened to friends of mine. It's called an 'extraction.'"

"Sounds like dental work."

"It can be a lot more painful than dental work, depending on the guy," said Sophie. "They bring pepper spray, handcuffs, rope, and a harness to lower you down. If you resist or don't cooperate, it can get pretty rough."

"I've had enough of these humans today," said Mal.

Mal and Sophie watched as the climber ran his chain around the redwood's huge trunk and then clipped each end to the sides of his harness. Facing the tree, he pulled the chain tight and drove his spikes into the bark. He leaned forward a bit to give the chain slack, then whipped it up a few feet higher. He leaned back on the chain for support and took another step up the trunk. Repeating the technique, he moved steadily upward, stabbing the tree with his spikes each time he progressed.

Sophie moved to the other side of the platform and reached down for something hanging from the trunk just below. With a groan she heaved it up and dropped it onto the platform with a loud bang. It was a heavy piece of steel pipe, actually two pipes welded together in a half circle.

"What's that, a pipe bomb?" asked Mal. "You gonna drop it on that dude?"

"It's a steel pipe lock box," said Sophie. "I'm going to hook it around this branch and lock my hands inside so no can get me out of this tree."

"You're serious, aren't you," said Mal.

Sophie said nothing as she lifted the pipe over the branch and began to lock her hands and arms inside. Mal peeked over the edge of the platform for reconnaissance on the climber. He had made swift progress and was now only about twenty feet below the platform.

Mal darted across the platform and grabbed the ugly metal toilet pot that hung from a lower branch. When he glanced back over the platform, the climber was now barely ten feet below. The climber looked up and his eyes locked on Mal in complete and utter surprise.

"Thou villainous, dog-hearted maltworm," said Mal, "come farther at thy peril."

"Hey, man, who are you? There's supposed to be just the girl," said the climber.

"Proceed one step thou reeky, beef-witted mold-warp, and thy goatish face shall be smitten with a terrible rain of excrement."

"Calm down, mister. Calm down," said the climber. "This ain't what I expected, so I'm gonna go back down just like you want."

Mal watched as the climber retreated, using his chain and spikes in reverse to quickly descend the tree. Sophie was still in her lock box, her arms raised over the branch, but staring at Mal in surprise.

"You just got involved. You just tried to make a difference. You just helped this tree survive," said Sophie.

"If I made any difference at all, it's probably just a matter of hours. Frustrating these humans only seems to make them more aggressive."

Sophie released herself from the lock box and sat down on the platform against the trunk. Mal looked down at the forest floor to make sure no one was there. Then he turned to Sophie.

"I'll tell you a little tale of frustration. I met this dude in the Blue Ridge Mountains not too long ago. He owned a big foam rubber factory and spent a lot of time figuring out a way to make foam rubber without using a nasty little chemical called 'penta.' It's a toxic flame retardant that's used in all kinds of things and it's been getting into everyone's bodies at higher and higher levels.

It's got the science guys very worried because it can cause brain damage in unborn babies and has even been found in the tissue of polar bears. The problem was that his non-toxic foam didn't have an even, consistent color, and because of that little cosmetic flaw nobody would buy it. So now we've got fire-proof polar bears on the tip of the iceberg of extinction while humans are melting the ice and poisoning both themselves and the planet."

"At least the foam guy *tried*, and maybe one day he'll succeed," said Sophie. "If everyone focused on one thing they care about, at least there's a chance of making the world a better place."

10

The Mission

THE SOUND OF CHAINS RATTLING BELOW made Mal and Sophie freeze. They stared at each other for a moment and then looked down to the ground. The climber was now with another man who looked even bigger and stronger. Both were wearing climbing harnesses and stretching out their long steel chains around the base of the trunk.

"He's back with reinforcements," said Mal.

Without saying a word, Sophie reached for the steel pipe lock box and began the cumbersome process of attaching herself to the tree.

"I'm not sure the toilet can tactic will work again this time," said Mal. "It's not exactly the most powerful weapon on earth. Not enough shock and awe."

The sound of chain links stretching out was followed by the thrusts of steel spikes into the tree. Then came the clattering whoosh of the chain being whipped up the tree trunk.

"Oh no, here they come," said Sophie.

The same set of sounds was heard again as the second climber followed behind. Mal glanced over the platform and saw it was the climber who had tried to visit before. The lead climber wore a backpack and a grim expression on his face.

Mal scanned the tiny platform, searching for an idea. The climbers were moving up fast, and he wasn't sure what to do. Sophie was now securely connected by steel pipe to the tree, determined never to leave. Mal could see no means of defense. The platform was hardly a fortress for repelling determined invaders, so Mal counterattacked with words.

"Thou craven, milk-livered measles, retreat or suffer mightily," Mal shouted.

The climbers stopped climbing for a moment, and the new lead climber yelled back.

"Don't worry, wing-nut, we're not comin' for you, even though you're trespassing. And the girl's got 'til tomorrow morning."

Mal didn't know what to make of what he heard or what the climbers were up to. He was sure it wasn't good, and they were quickly getting closer.

He looked over at Sophie. Her eyes were softly closed. She seemed to be meditating. Her arms were raised above her inside the curved steel pipe that locked her around a thick jutting branch in a strangely awkward embrace. She looked like a volunteer hostage to the tree she was trying to save. She also looked afraid.

The sounds of the whipping chains and thrusting spikes were getting louder and that meant closer. Mal didn't look down, but stared out across the forest. His eyes were still and focused as he thought about what he could do. Now, Mal looked down over the platform and saw the climbers a few feet below.

"By the sword of Saint Julian thou shall suffer, thou spleeny, toad-spotted scuts," Mal shouted with great authority.

There was no response, just silence, and then the sound of a zipper. Mal stared intently across the forest, and soon he heard another sound.

"Vvvvvvveeeeeeeeeeeeeeeeeeeeeeeeeeeeeeeeeeee eeeeeeeeee."

Mal stuck his head out over the edge again. The big lead climber was ripping away at the platform with a battery-powered saw. Mal instantly turned to Sophie.

"Get out of that pipe! They're cutting the floor out from under us!"

Sophie opened her eyes in a flash and realized it was true. She unlocked herself from the steel pipe and angrily hurled it down to the ground.

"Vvvvvvveeeeeeeeeeeeeeeeeeeeeeeeeeeeeeeeeeee eeeeeeeeee."

Mal and Sophie saw the saw blade rapidly cutting up through the plywood where they sat.

"This tree house is history," said Mal. "We gotta get outta here."

"Vvvvvvveeeeeeeeeeeeeeeeeeeeeeeeeeeeeeeeeeeeee eeeeeeeeee."

Sophie sprang into action. She jumped up and reached for a branch above her and began to climb up the tree. Mal was right on her heels, climbing as fast as he could.

About twenty feet above the platform, Sophie stopped and looked back. It forced Mal to stop and do the same. They could hear the saw, but they couldn't see the climbers who were still work-ing beneath the plywood. Then with a crack of splintering wood, they watched the platform break away and fall and spin like a leaf down toward the forest floor. Everything was gone.

The climbers were visible now as they too watched the platform dropping to the ground. Then they looked up at Mal and Sophie. The big lead climber broke into a smile and shouted at them.

"Have a nice day, tree-huggers."

Sophie looked up to where she wanted to go and didn't say a word. A sad expression washed over Mal's face as he continued to climb.

"Humans. What a species," he thought to himself.

Sophie began to climb even faster. Mal tried hard to keep pace, being careful not to slip and fall. He knew exactly where Sophie was headed, her favorite place in the tree.

After a few more minutes, Sophie reached the lightning cave. Mal was not far behind, and when he climbed up within sight of the cave, he saw the tears streaming from Sophie's eyes. The stress and shock of what had happened was taking its toll on her, unleashing pent-up emotions. Mal thought of it as "battle fatigue."

"It's not easy to see your home destroyed," said Mal.

"This whole tree is my home, and the lumber company won't be happy until they've destroyed it too."

"The world seems hell-bent on destruction these days," said Mal.

"But it doesn't have to be that way. It's not the world I want, and I know it's not the world that you want either."

Sophie wiped the tears from her eyes.

"I hate to say it," she said, "but maybe you were right. Trying to save this tree may always have been futile."

"*I* hate to say it, but *you're* the one who's right. You're brave and you're committed and you're trying to make a difference. That's what really counts, and you deserve a medal of valor."

"What counts is saving this tree," said Sophie.

Mal thought for a moment before he replied.

"Losing a battle here and there doesn't mean you can't win the war."

11

The Wrath

STANDING ON A BRANCH NEXT TO SOPHIE, who was nestled in her lightning cave, Mal gazed out over the forest. The sun was getting lower and redder and beginning to throw shafts of "God's light" at an angle through the trees.

"You know you have to face it," said Mal. "It's probably part of human nature to be short-sighted, to not see the forest for the trees."

Sophie calmly braced herself for what seemed like the prelude to another one of Mal's rants.

"When humans started polluting the air with factories and machines, they had no idea they'd change the planet's climate. That was only a hundred and fifty years ago, the so-called 'Industrial Revolution.' That was when humans started becoming the first species in history to be a force of nature.

Now that humans *are* a force of nature, they *have* to look at the bigger picture, the whole forest and not just the trees. They *have* to *change* their ways. They have to stop charging blindly ahead and figure out a decent retreat from their mindless destruction of nature. Otherwise we're truly facing the beginning of the end of the world, or at least the world as we know it.

You know, the Pope has said that pollution is a modern-day sin. 'Thou shall honor thy Mother Earth' should be a new commandment.

We need another revolution, a battle on the side of nature.

There's a basic law of nature that says any species that fouls its environment and reduces the chances of its offspring flourishing is on the road to extinction."

"I don't think you really believe the human race is doomed," said Sophie.

"You and I may be doomed right now. No food, no water, no platform, not even a rope to get down."

"So, what do you think that Jesus would say to do?" asked Sophie.

"Oh, he'd probably say to put your faith in God and surrender to his will, but you said surrender wasn't an option."

Sophie scooted over in the cave and motioned to Mal to share the seat. They watched the sun set and a full moon rise, and neither said a word for a while. They were stranded in the redwood tree, each hoping for an inspiration for how they would survive.

Dusk turned to darkness lighted by the moon. The forest was eerily beautiful, but Mal and Sophie were starting to feel the cold.

Suddenly, from the forest floor, came the sound of something moving. Mal's ears went on full alert, trying to make out what it was, an animal or a human. Sophie listened intently too and shook her head sideways to Mal, signaling she couldn't tell what the sound was either. From the greater height of the lightning cave, it was harder to hear or see what was going on below, especially at night.

"BrrruunngguuunnngguuunnnRrrrrraaaaaaaaaaaaaaaaaaaahhh."

The sound of a chainsaw firing up shattered the quiet of the forest.

"Holy Shiite," said Mal.

"I don't believe this," said Sophie.

"Rrrrrrrrrrrrraaaaaaaaaaaaaaaaaaaaaaaaaaaaaaaahhhhhhhhhh."

Mal slid off the lip of the cave and climbed out on a branch to get a better look at what was happening below. In the glow of the moonlight he saw it.

"Some human is trying to cut this tree down," said Mal.

"*This* tree?"

"Yeah, this tree," said Mal.

"Somebody's out of their mind."

"Rrrrrrrrrrrrraaaaaaaaaaaaaaaaaaaaaaaaaaaaaaa aahhhhhhhhh."

Sophie scampered out of the cave.

"I just had an idea," she said. "Follow me."

As he climbed down behind Sophie in the darkness, Mal sensed whoever was down there wasn't fooling around. This wasn't psychological warfare, waged to strike fear and terror. From the unrelenting sound of the chainsaw, Mal had little doubt that this was a vicious deliberate attack. The target was the tree and anyone who was in it.

"Rrrrrrrrrrrrraaaaaaaaaaaaaaaaaaaaaaaaaaaaaaa aahhhhhhhhh."

Suddenly Sophie came to a halt and sat on a thick jutting branch. As Mal descended closer, he saw the two lengths of rope that extended across to the neighboring tree where Sophie's boyfriend's platform remained. The ropes were the traverse lines he had asked about before, the ropes from which Sophie's boyfriend had fallen to his death. In their panic to abandon their platform, both Sophie and Mal had overlooked a possible way to escape.

"These lines are old and they could break, but this is our only chance," said Sophie. "Stand on the low one and hold the top one tight and slowly work your way over with little sidesteps."

"No, no. Ladies first. I insist. Get yourself off this deathtrap," said Mal. "Plus, I wanna see how it's done."

"Rrrrrrrrrrrrrraaaaaaaaaaaaaaaaaaaaaaaaaaa aaaaahhhhhhhhh."

Whoever had the chainsaw was working hard and fast. Sophie grabbed the top rope, then stood on the lower one, and began to carefully work her way across at more than two hundred feet above the forest floor. The bottom rope bowed and swayed from her weight, bending more with each step. Halfway there, she turned her head to look back at Mal standing anxiously on the large branch and trying to hold the top rope taut. They shared quick nervous smiles.

"Rrrrrrrrrrrrrraaaaaaaaaaaaaaaaaaaaaaaaaaa aaaaaahhhhhhhhh."

Moving a little faster now, Sophie shuffled the rest of the way in nearly half the time. Finally, she stepped onto the rickety platform and turned to look back at Mal.

"Rrrrrrrrrrrrrraaaaaaaaaaaaaaaaaaaaaaaaaaa aaaaahhhhhhhhh."

The chainsaw let out another scream followed by the aching sound of splintering, cracking wood. The tree cutter below had accomplished the murderous mission. The redwood started to fall.

Sophie watched in silent horror as Mal clung to the tree, riding it down into the darkness as it swept ever faster toward the ground and slammed onto the forest floor.

12

The Miracle

SOPHIE STOOD FROZEN IN SHOCK AT THE atrocity she had witnessed. She felt her legs go weak and then she buckled onto the shaky platform. She began to cry. Tears at first. Then sobs. In moments she was wailing, screaming out across the forest dappled by the light of the moon.

Her mind flashed back to the freakish death of her boyfriend. Then other images raced through her head, images of redwoods falling and of her tiny wooden platform spinning down toward the forest floor. Then she re-lived the sight of Mal holding on to her tree as it toppled to the ground. The stress of the day and the trauma of Mal's murder left her completely shattered.

After a long while, she began to calm down. She took deep breaths and meditated, searching for the focus she had lost. Slowly clarity was restored, her concentration returned, her survival instincts took hold. With the full-faced moon now high above, she carefully scanned the platform.

There was nothing to see, until she glanced at the trunk of the tree itself. Hanging from a stub of a branch, she noticed an old coiled climbing rope covered with dirt and cobwebs. It was a godsend that offered the means for Sophie to make her way down.

She stepped lightly across the creaky platform, unsure if it would hold. Suspended and tethered by old rotting ropes, the plywood teetered as she shifted her weight. Sophie stopped dead and regained her balance. A few more cautious steps and she was there. She clutched the tree's trunk with one hand and grabbed the rope with the other.

Slowly, Sophie sat down and began uncoiling the rope. She wrapped one end around a sturdy branch and secured it with a bowline knot she knew wouldn't slip or give way.

Sophie took another deep breath and gently closed her eyes. She began to meditate once again. She knew she needed all her strength of mind for the long and sad climb down, and she needed new strength of spirit. She had promised herself not to set foot on ground until her tree was saved. But that was now a lost cause, just as Mal had predicted.

After a few minutes, Sophie opened her eyes and peered down over the platform. Then she looked up at the sky, and felt lucky for the night's full moon. A descent in total darkness would have been foolishly dangerous if not impossible, but in the glowing moonlight she believed she had a chance of coming down alive.

Sophie grabbed the rope tightly and carefully lowered her foot onto a branch just below. With one foot firmly planted, her other foot followed from the wobbly platform. Standing on only the tree made her feel safer, and she began to slowly descend.

Step by step, she clambered down, holding onto branches with one hand while the other gripped the rope, which she prayed was not so rotted it would snap and send her falling. She dropped her foot to another branch and it slipped off a patch of wet moss. Sophie suddenly lost her balance as well as her grip on the tree. Her free hand flailed away from the tree but managed to grasp the rope. With both hands she clung to it desperately as it stretched and recoiled from her weight but luckily didn't break.

Hanging on for her life, hands burning from her slipping grip, Sophie extended a leg toward a branch and pulled herself back to the tree. She hooked her leg over the branch, and in a sudden burst of power swung herself on top of it while clinging to the rope. Living in her tree had made her strong.

Face down on the saving branch, her arms and legs wrapped around it, Sophie looked like a sloth sleeping in a rainforest. Like a sloth, she stayed still and rested, trying to recover strength and composure from her death-defying ordeal. The night was cold but Sophie didn't feel it. She embraced the tree for more than an hour.

"WhoooooWhooooo."

The call of an owl echoed through the forest and reminded Sophie she was alive. The shock of nearly dying had begun to subside, and she knew it was time to continue her climb down. She pushed herself up into a sitting position, her legs still straddling the branch, and reached for the dangling rope. She pulled it taut and took a long deep breath.

Gripping the rope, Sophie scooted forward until she reached the tree's trunk. With the rope as support, she dismounted the branch and carefully stepped down to a lower limb. Slowly and deliberately, she resumed her retreat from the tree, using branches as her stairway until the branches ran out and only the massive trunk extended to the ground.

In the moonlight, Sophie could see that the rope nearly reached the ground. She took it as a sign that her luck was holding, and began the final leg down, slowly stepping backwards along the trunk with the rope as her only support. Her arms ached and her hands seemed on fire as she drew on every last bit of her strength.

At six feet above the forest floor, Sophie reached the end of the rope. She clutched it tightly, let her feet drop off the trunk, and hung suspended by her hands for a second before she let go and dropped to the ground. She rolled sideways as she landed and sprawled onto her back, looking straight up at the tree and the sky.

Sophie took a deep breath and rolled onto her side. It was then when she saw the huge stump of the tree she had tried so hard to save. She couldn't tell quite what she was feeling as she stared at it in the moonlight, but she didn't shed a tear. Now she sat up and saw the rest of her tree, a fallen giant in eerie silhouette.

"Mal?" Sophie said to herself as she got onto her feet and ran toward the tree. She stopped at the severed end of the trunk and touched and smelled the moist pungent wood. Then she walked slowly along the tree, stepping over shattered limbs, looking for some sign of Mal.

In a pool of moonlight, she saw him, lying lifeless atop the trunk, bloody, bruised and lacerated, his arms stretched out to his sides. His eyes were wide open staring to the stars. Strangely, there was a smile on his face.

Sophie dropped to her knees and began to cry uncontrollably. The tragedy before her was too much to bear. Her tree was gone and Mal was dead. She knew she was willing to die for her tree, but it hurt her deeply that it was Mal who had made the ultimate sacrifice.

In a rising flood of grief and despair, Sophie began to experience the grudging, yet honest affection that had grown in her for Mal. She had never known quite what to make of him, and assumed he was half crazy, but Mal had become a friend. It was then that Sophie realized what she had come to admire about Mal. It was something also a part of her. Something they shared. Something she thought of as passion.

The sound of a twig breaking caught Sophie's attention. A flash of fear surged through her as she froze and carefully listened. Now, she heard the crunch of footsteps moving across the forest floor. The footsteps grew ever louder. Someone or something was approaching.

Sophie felt another pang of fear. She realized Mal's killer might still be in the forest. Suddenly, a beam of light swept across her face. Sophie instantly hit the ground and crawled toward her fallen tree. She tried to hide beside the trunk, but worried it was too late.

"Come out, tree-hugger, wherever you are," a man's voice taunted.

Now the light shined directly in her face. Looming above her was Bigfoot. Bigfoot then panned his flashlight along the trunk of the tree.

He stopped when he saw Mal's body and held the light on it for a while.

As Bigfoot slowly moved closer to get a better look, Sophie got up and silently followed.

"I've seen this guy before. I tried to arrest him. He's a fugitive from the law. Anyway, he used to be."

"Did you do this?" Sophie demanded, "Or one of your goons?"

Bigfoot shot Sophie a withering glare.

"This forest can be a dangerous place," said Bigfoot as he pointed his flashlight back onto Mal.

"Especially with you in it," said Sophie.

"I'm gonna get the sheriff. And the coroner. You're comin' with me."

With that Sophie bolted. She dashed away into the forest, running as fast as she could, desperately fleeing Bigfoot.

"Hey, tree-hugger, you won't get away!" Bigfoot yelled after her. "My boys'll track you down at dawn."

Bigfoot didn't bother to chase Sophie. He had a dead man to deal with. He shined his flashlight on Mal once again. Then he turned and tromped away into the darkness of the forest.

Sophie had hidden herself fairly close by, crouched behind a nurse log and under a giant fern. She waited quietly for a while, until she felt sure that Bigfoot was really gone. Then she walked cautiously back to Mal and her tree.

Tears filled Sophie's eyes as she stepped closer to where Mal was lying. She placed her finger on his wrist, feeling for a pulse. There was nothing. She gazed at his smiling face and closed his open eyes. She kissed him on the forehead.

A moment later, Sophie witnessed something unbelievable. Slowly at first but ever-faster, Mal began to change. The blood on his body evaporated. His scrapes and cuts and bruises healed. His beard disappeared. His hair turned dark and thick. His skin lost all its wrinkles. His muscles bulged with new strength. Sophie gasped and held her breath. Before her eyes, Mal transformed into a different person. It was like watching time flow backward as Sophie witnessed Mal transfigure into a younger and younger man.

Awestruck and stunned and speechless, Sophie simply stared at the strikingly handsome new young Mal lying on the trunk of her fallen tree. He slowly opened his eyes and blinked several times as if waking up. Then he turned his head to Sophie and smiled.

"I'm back," said Mal.

Sophie looked like she'd seen a ghost.

She gazed at Mal in wonderment, contemplating the miracle of what had just occurred. She felt like part of a fairy tale where magic turns an ugly frog into a charming prince. Finally, Sophie spoke.

"Mal? Is that you? What just happened? Am I hallucinating? What's going on?"

"I can tell you didn't believe me," said Mal.

"Believe that you've been walking the earth since the time of Jesus Christ? Can you blame me?"

"I told you all about it," said Mal. "I was cursed to walk the earth until the world ends. Most humans are afraid of death, but I don't have that problem. I've got the burden of immortality, and believe me, it's not easy."

"So if you die, you're born again?"

"Kind of," said Mal. "If I don't get killed along the way, I live to be sixty. Then I come back as an eighteen-year-old and start all over again. Rejuvenation. Been doing it for centuries, and believe me, it's depressing seeing the world get worse and worse."

"But it doesn't have to be that way," said Sophie.

"That's what I really admire about you. You never give up on your ideals. So listen, I've got a new plan. I'm living this life differently. I'm gonna get involved. I'm gonna try to change things for the better. I'm gonna try to save the world from going where it's headed. And I want to do it with you."

Sophie simply stared at Mal in utter disbelief.

"If you believe in the ultimate power of one person to make a difference," said Mal, "imagine the power of two."

Sophie continued to stare.

"I'll tell ya what," said Mal. "Now's the time to get out of here, before we get arrested. And I know just where to go. It's an ancient, gorgeous wilderness that needs a helping hand. There are folks who want to exploit it for profit, and if they get their way, they'll pretty much ruin the place. You could be an activist and try to stop the madness, and I'd be right there with you fighting on the side of nature."

"Where is this place?" asked Sophie.

"It's east of here in Utah, around a town called Moab. A town named after an ancient place not far from Jerusalem where I was born. It's a place of red rivers and rapids and canyons and arches and spires. It's a grand natural cathedral, covered with pinion and juniper and countless wild flowers. It's a land full of magic. A place I think you'll love."

"Moab?"

"Here, we'll be thrown in jail," said Mal.

Sophie looked deeply into the eyes of the new, reborn young Mal. She seemed bewildered and confused, but then after a time, a smile spread over her beautiful face. It was the glowing, knowing smile of someone who'd had an epiphany, who had experienced something divine. Finally, Sophie spoke.

"All right, let's go to Moab."

Sophie took a final look at her beloved tree, and then she slowly turned away, tears streaming from her eyes.

In the misty predawn light, Mal and Sophie began to walk. Soon after they left the fallen tree behind, they spotted a thicket of wild berries. They picked them and ate them until they were full, and then continued their journey.

When Bigfoot returned to where he'd found Mal, he found himself in trouble. The sheriff had come with him, along with the county coroner, and so had the cub reporter, as well as a handful of Green Earth activists. Soon everyone had questions that Bigfoot couldn't answer.

Where was the body of the man, the dead "fugitive from the law" who Bigfoot said he had found? What happened to the young tree-sitter? Why had she also disappeared? Who cut down the redwood in the middle of the night? Why couldn't Bigfoot's security team prevent such a thing from happening?

The story hit the papers:

TREE SITTER MURDER MYSTERY
Lumber Company Questioned

TREE SITTERS DEAD OR MISSING?
Sheriffs Searching for Clues

The headlines and the story captured great public attention. Green Earth held a large rally and demanded a full investigation. The sheriff's office was baffled, and soon the district attorney became involved. Confronted with growing pressure, the lumber company agreed that logging would be halted in that section of the forest until the mystery was solved, until the events of that fateful night could be adequately explained.

An explanation would never come. The mystery would never be solved. No one ever knew what happened to Sophie and Mal.

The forest where Sophie's redwood fell would never be cut down.

As the sun rose and shined its warming light upon them, Mal and Sophie continued their exodus east, over high mountains and across a vast desert toward the place called Moab.

In the days when Jesus walked the earth, "Moab" meant "a beautiful land."

Epilogue

IN MOAB, MAL AND SOPHIE HELPED STOP a destructive project to drill for natural gas amid the ancient, pristine red rock canyons of the region. Then they walked south to the Navajo Nation and worked to contain the deadly pollution from abandoned uranium mines. They traveled north to Alaska to rescue birds and other creatures threatened by an oil spill.

In Brazil, they fought beside others to save the dwindling rainforests. On islands in the South Pacific, they devoted themselves to the struggle of saving threatened coral reefs. In Africa, they joined the campaign to protect endangered mountain gorillas from being slaughtered into extinction.

For untold years they roamed the earth, working to make it a better place. They devoted their lives to making a difference, and lived happily ever after.

19835814R00080

Made in the USA
Charleston, SC
14 June 2013